HARBINGER: ANCIENT PURGE BOOK 0

M.C. BASS

ZARTANIA SYSTEMS, LLC

BOOKS IN THE ANCIENT PURGE SERIES

Don't miss out on the next book in the series! **Visit the following link** and I'll let you know when it's available!
http://mcbassauthor.com/letmeknow

Book 0 - Harbinger
Book 1 - Awakening
Book 2 - Evolution
Book 3 - Discovery (Coming soon)

PROLOGUE

Godfrey Bennett couldn't sleep, so he picked up a candle from the table beside his bed and lit it. Then, he walked down the grand staircase and into his first-floor library. Bennett sat the candle on the table by his chair, picked up the iron poker and stoked the dying fire before sitting heavily in the high-backed leather chair near the fireplace. He sat there several minutes, mind whirling with business decisions he would make the next day to increase his family's considerable wealth. Satisfied that his business affairs were going to be in order for the next day, he allowed himself to relax and let his mind wander. After several minutes of random thought, he closed his eyes and willed sleep to take him because he was exhausted from the many recent, sleepless nights. Several seconds passed, and just as sleep started to take him, he was jolted fully awake by a loud clicking noise that sounded from behind him. He stood up and walked over to the intricately carved walnut bookcases and searched for the offending noise.

A stone chest that had been in his family for centuries glowed a soft, orange hue. He approached the chest slowly. It was mysterious to him because he could never decipher how to open it, nor could previous generations of his family. But now, he could see a slight space between the chest and its lid. He placed both hands on either end of the lid and felt the warmth emanating from it. He lifted it gently and carefully laid it to rest next to the chest. When he peered into the chest he jumped back because he thought that he saw something moving within the chest.

Frightened, but not deterred, he retrieved the candle from the table beside his chair. Then, he walked back over to the chest and held the candle high so that he could see the contents. Indeed, there was something black moving within the chest; almost like sand. His curiosity overtook him and he dipped his fingers into the blackness. Instantly, the blackness moved quickly up his arm and began entering his eyes, ears, nose, and mouth. He cried out in horror, dropped the candle, and started swatting at the blackness with his hands. The candle caught the draperies on fire, and fire rose quickly up the drapes and began to spread across the ceiling. He didn't notice though, because he was still swatting at the writhing, black mass that now covered his entire body. He tried to scream but found that he couldn't. Then, he felt intense pain deep inside his head before his world went black and he collapsed to the floor amongst the flames.

His body convulsed and his joints cracked as the blackness overtook over his body. Then, as quickly as it had begun, it ended, and his eyes opened. Black eyes, with no white. He stood with flames still burning all around him and walked through them, blistering his exposed skin. He stopped at the front door and stood still, cocking his head to the side, almost as if listening to something, and then he opened the door. Suddenly, he bolted through the open door and ran into the night, straight into the heart of London. He ran through the city that night spreading the blackness to everyone that crossed his path by biting them. He continued for hours, then stopped suddenly. Then, he turned and ran back to his house, which was now nothing more than a smoldering pile. He waded into the wreckage to the spot where his library had once been and started digging with his hands. His skin began to blister and fall off in sizzling chunks, yet he continued to dig. After several seconds, he pulled the stone chest free with his now skeletal hands. The lid on the chest opened slightly and the blackness flowed out of his body and back into the chest. Then the lid closed, and Godfrey Bennett fell into the smoldering ashes. His normal, pale blue eyes stared lifelessly at the sky as his fleshed melted into the embers.

~

Eleven days later, death cart laborers worked throughout the night to dig the huge mass graves. Some of them wore lavender-soaked rags over their noses to combat the smell of death and burnt flesh that lingered in the air all around them. Bodies were stacked in rows like cord-wood and went on for as far as the eye could see. Some pits were freshly dug and lay empty, awaiting the bodies that would surely come. Others were half full of dead bodies but were filling quickly as more dead were carted over and dumped into them. Some of the pits smoldered from the fires that had been set in them to try to kill the black death.

Minister Hughes stood on the street corner nearest the pits and rubbed his aching finger. A small child had bitten him a few hours ago as he tried to deliver his message to the people. The embarrassed mother jerked the child away and apologized profusely, but the damage was done. She had bitten him so hard that she had drawn blood. Angered, but still determined, he resumed his sermon of God's vengeance. This pestilence was payment for their sins. The people of London had strayed too far from God, and now they would suffer the consequences. Only the believers and righteous would be spared. He had repeated this same sermon several times per day, each day since the pestilence had struck London.

Minister Hughes was about to repeat his sermon for the fifth time that day when his head started to hurt. Then he started coughing violently. The crowd began to back away from him in fear that he too, was sick. He raised his hand to his mouth out of habit as he coughed. He looked at his hand and was horrified to see black blood dripping from his fingers. Apparently, he was a sinner too.

. . .

3

One-third of the European population died in 1348. History tells us that it was the Bubonic Plague, also known as The Black Death. But, history is wrong. It was something far worse...

1

Present Day - subterranean cavern off the coast of Alexandria, Egypt.

Double agent Eli Cohen spat on the dead Arab who lay at his feet.

"Fuck you, pig!"

The man had emerged from the pool at the end of the cavern—the same one Eli had swum through only minutes earlier. The struggle had lasted several minutes, and now Eli breathed heavily as sweat ran down his forehead and stung his eyes. He shook his head and muttered, "Either I'm losing my skills or everyone else is getting better. That was way too much effort."

He snapped photographs of the dead Arab's face and then undressed the man, noting every detail, from tattoos to the jewelry he wore. Any of it might be important in identifying him and what group he worked for.

Eli was an Israeli Mossad agent, but his true allegiance was with the Orion Society. They didn't hold prejudice against any race or nation, which was something Eli struggled with, because as a child, he was taught to hate the Arab nations. The Orion Society was formed in 212 AD to protect the earth, and to make sure everything remained harmonious. They were a combination of all races and religions, and preferred peace over violence. As long as peace didn't threaten the extinction of the human race.

He looked across the cavern and stared at the perfectly preserved body of someone he didn't recognize, mesmerized by the transparent sarcophagus. He pulled up the sleeve of his dive suit and checked his smart watch, then frowned when he realized that he didn't have a signal. He wanted to reach the elders to see if there was anything else he should take with him. Sighing with frustration, he settled for taking pictures and video of the cavern. The elders could decide what they wanted to do later.

He turned his attention to the golden ring in the palm of his hand. King Solomon's ring, or that's what the elders had said anyway. They had told Eli that it was the same ring that King Solomon used to control demons and make them build a temple in God's honor. Eli scoffed at the idea. Even though he grew up in a very religious family, he'd had other ideas about life since he had attended college and joined the Mossad. And he had really started to doubt his faith after all of the missions he'd been on for the Orion Society during the last three years. His missions mainly consisted of retrieving old documents, either in the form of scrolls or animal skins lashed together with leather cords. Never a ring though, or any type of treasure, until now. The ring shone brightly in the light of his head lamp as he rotated it in the palm of his hand.

He laughed softly and said, "I understand going after the documents. There was probably important knowledge in them. But this? An old gold ring with the Star of David and a red jewel. I don't understand."

Emboldened by his self-talk, he placed the ring on his finger. Immediately he felt surges of electricity run up and down his limbs, and a strange humming sensation filled his head. He dropped to his knees in agony and tried to remove the ring, but it was stuck. His eyes widened, and he became frantic as he struggled with the ring.

He shouted out of habit, "God help me!"

The demon said, "He already has. That's why you have the ring. I wouldn't ask again if I were you. Yahweh has been known to lose His patience in the presence of fools."

Eli looked up and stared in horror at the grotesque form before him. The demon was so large that it couldn't stand fully erect in the cavern. It stared at Eli with soulless, black eyes.

The demon laughed and said, "What's the matter, Eli Cohen? Are you afraid of me?"

Eli stuttered, "N-no! Leave me alone!"

He blinked, and the demon was gone. Bewildered, he looked around frantically and questioned his sanity. He looked down at the ring and tugged on it again to try to remove it, but it remained stuck on his finger.

"I'm over here, fool," a smooth, female voice crooned.

Eli spun his head and saw a beautiful, naked woman walk out from behind the tomb of Alexander the Great. Her long, blonde hair cascaded down her shoulders and onto her ample breasts. Eli's eyes traveled up and down her athletic body and then settled on her deep, blue eyes. The longer he looked into her eyes, the more he wanted her. But instead of acting on his desire, he broke the trance and instead stared at the glass tomb.

"Am I easier on your eyes now?"

The demon pointed at the tomb. "He wasn't so great, you know. That Alexander guy. After all, he died just like the rest of you do. Do you want to die, Eli? I wonder what would happen if you did. Your faith is weak. You're weak. You're all weak.

"Take me with you out of this place or I'll kill you. Actually, I could kill you right now, and that ring wouldn't protect you because you don't believe. You're not worthy enough to be wearing King Solomon's ring. In fact, I'm surprised that Yahweh Himself hasn't already killed you."

His father had taught Eli and his siblings about demons during their daily studies of the Torah. However, Eli had never believed such a thing existed and thought his father was a religious fanatic. In fact, he didn't really believe in God at all, but now, he wasn't sure about anything, and that terrified him. Eli's mind raced as he tried to come up with a plan.

He could think of only one thing, and it was something his father had taught all of his children. Eli mustered his courage and faced the beautiful woman who now stood only feet from him.

"In the name of Yahweh! Be gone and harass me no more!"

The beautiful woman turned back into the heinous creature, and it cried out in rage. Then it vanished before Eli's eyes.

King Solomon's ring fell from his finger and landed on the sandy floor.

Eli stood still and stared at the ring, then closed his eyes and said a prayer of thanks. He gingerly picked up the ring and placed it in a pouch on his dive belt.

He scanned the cavern and whispered to himself, "I don't know if any of what I think I saw actually happened or not, but I'm not sticking around for a replay. Time to go."

Eli shrugged into his rebreather and placed the fitting in his mouth. Then he pulled his face mask down and dove into the pool at the end of the cavern. The gravity of what had happened dawned on him as he swam through the cave. He felt a sense of renewed respect for the elders and the Orion Society's mission. Anyone who possessed the ring could use it for creation, like King Solomon did when he built the temple, or for destruction. He shuddered at the thought of someone unleashing an army of demons.

He paused as he neared the mouth of the cave that would take him back into the Mediterranean Sea. He reasoned that if the Arab wasn't working alone, there would likely be others in the area, waiting to take his head off as soon as he surfaced. So, Eli swam beneath the surface and followed the coastline of Alexandria. He checked the navigation system on his smart watch and notified his partner, Olivia Berg, that he would be diverting from their original pickup location. Then he turned on his beacon, which would allow her to find him, and kicked hard with his fins, knifing through the water like a porpoise. Minutes later, he breached the water's surface near an old, faded-blue fishing boat and swam toward it.

When he reached the boat, a gloved hand reached for him to offer assistance. Eli looked up into the face of an Arab man, wriggled free of his grip, and was about to dive when he heard a familiar voice.

"Hello, idiot! Pretty good disguise, huh? It took about an hour to get it right. Would you like some help getting into the boat now?" Olivia said.

Slightly embarrassed, Eli took the offered hand and pulled himself into the boat. He stared at her, taking in every detail of her disguise. She was a true master. A full wig and beard accompanied an artful makeup job. The brown wig she wore covered her Nordic blonde hair and looked completely natural. He stared into her brown eyes and found it difficult, because he knew they were normally a beautiful ice-blue color.

Eli said, "Damn, you're good. You've managed to take an absolutely gorgeous face and turn it into an ugly Arab guy." He smirked. "Strangely, you remind me of a Saudi friend of mine, Ahmed. Not that he's ugly or anything. Anyway, that's the name I'm giving you while you're in that disguise. Hey, speaking of disguises, did you bring anything for me?"

"You're such a prick sometimes, Eli!" Olivia huffed as she pulled a duffel bag from behind the wheel housing and handed it to him. He unzipped it and peered inside. "Nice! I'm sure it has everything that I need to get into disguise, but before I do that, I need to get rid of the evidence."

Eli began removing his dive gear and tossing it over the side of the boat into the harbor. He removed the pouch from his dive belt and zipped it open, making sure the ring was still secure. Every time he looked at it or touched it, he had an uneasy feeling. The same feeling that he'd had when the demon confronted and tormented him.

Once he had disposed of all of his dive gear, he began pulling the contents of the disguise bag out and laying them on a wooden bench attached to the boat's hull. He washed his hands thoroughly and then put the brown contact lenses into his eyes, effectively covering his natural blue color. Next came the fake black beard and wig to cover his sandy-colored hair. When he finished gluing the beard onto his face, he turned to Olivia and cleared his throat to get her attention. "How do I look, Ahmed?"

Olivia smirked and said, "Convincing, but not as good as I look. In addition to being a beautiful woman, I think I even make a pretty nice-looking Arab guy. Don't you think?" She winked at him and laughed as she piloted the boat back into the harbor, then angled for one of the many canals running through Alexandria.

Eli said, "Yeah, yeah, I hear you, princess. Did you find us a safe location to ditch this boat and switch disguises?"

"Yes, see that canal up ahead? It's right off of it. The building is a bit run-down, but we won't be there long anyway. And the bonus is that it hasn't been used in a very long time. I've also taken the standard safe house protocol and rigged everything up. We'll know if anyone has been there since I left to come and pick you up. We're good. I've taken care of things. You should trust me a little more, you know?"

Eli laughed and ran his fingers through his fake beard. "The last time I trusted you we almost died!"

She reached for his hand, pulled him over, and kissed him gently. "I think we were both distracted. It wasn't entirely my fault. I'll assume fifty percent responsibility and no more than that. You can take the other half."

Eli put his arm around her, leaned over, and whispered in her ear, "You know what they would do to us in this country if they saw two guys kissing? Nothing good, I assure you. Now, about that fifty percent. You know what we're doing is against Orion Society rules, right? In fact, it's rule number two. 'No society members shall have intimate relationships with one another. No exceptions.' So, not only are we breaking the rules, but this is dangerous. If an enemy of the Society caught either one of us, and they knew we had a relationship, they would use that against us in interrogation. Honestly, in the two months we've been together, I've fallen for you, Olivia.

"We've worked together many times before, and I was never attracted to you like I am now. This isn't something I planned or even dreamed of, but it's happened nonetheless, and I'm very happy about that!"

Eli paused and then stuttered, "I-I-I'm in love with you!"

Olivia reached up and wiped a tear away from her right eye as it threatened to cascade down into her fake beard. Then, suddenly, she reached under the console and thrust a rope into Eli's hand, then shoved him with her hip.

"Look like you're busy. There's a man waving at us from the dock on the front of the canal we need to travel down. You're right, we have to keep our distance or we'll blow our cover."

She smiled and said, "Hey, just so you know, I love you too."

Their eyes met and desire flared in both of them, only to be interrupted by the man calling to them in Arabic from a nearby dock.

Olivia frowned and said, "Eli, we have to respond to him, and you have to do all of the talking. There wasn't any vocal cord spray in the disguise kit for me to use to deepen my voice."

As they neared the man, Eli waved and called out in Arabic. It turned out that all the man wanted to know was whether they had caught any fish. Eli quickly told him that the fishing wasn't good that evening while they slipped slowly by him and traveled up the crowded canal.

Olivia squinted through the dimly lit canal and spotted a dock close to the building they'd use to change into their next disguises and wait for their ride to the airport. She expertly steered the small boat toward it and gently bumped against the dock. Eli tied the small boat to a dock cleat, then gathered their bags and tossed them onto the dock. They stood on the dock, exchanged a glance, and then slung their bags over their shoulders and pulled out their pistols. Eli stood on one side of the doorway and Olivia on the other. She gave him a nod. He slung the door open and stepped quickly inside, sweeping to the right. Olivia followed him in and immediately swept to the left.

"Clear!" Eli said and moved into the next room.

Olivia said, "Clear!" And followed Eli into the adjacent room. It was so small that they didn't bother with the standard room-clearing talk and instead began undressing.

Olivia stripped out of her men's Arab clothing, but left the dark contact lenses in her eyes. Their plan was to leave Egypt disguised as a wealthy Arab couple, which allowed them to fly out in a private jet and not raise any suspicions.

Eli stripped out of his fisherman's disguise and walked up behind Olivia's lithe body, put his arms around her, and gently nibbled at her neck. She moaned, but put her hands on his and slowly pried them away.

"It's too dangerous here, and you know it. This is not the place, Eli. We need to change and get the hell out of here as quickly as possible."

Eli grumbled, kissed her on the cheek, and resumed putting together his new disguise. But then he sighed heavily and said, "Yeah, I know it's too dangerous here. You know, I'm really getting sick of this job. Hell, it's not even my real job. It sounded cool when my father told me our family had been a part of the Orion Society for hundreds of years and it was my responsibility to continue our family legacy. But what if I don't want to? I know I'm stuck in the Mossad for life. The only way I'll be leaving there is if I'm dead, or too old to do the job. But, I wonder, can we get out of the Orion Society and live happily ever after, or would they kill us?"

Olivia reached up, straightened his wig, and said, "I don't know, but I don't want to find out either. My story is similar to yours. My family has also been in the Orion Society for hundreds of years. However, the difference between you and me is that I want to be a part of the Orion Society. I think maybe your problem is that you're working too much. I don't have the same schedule on the Swedish Special Forces that you do with the Mossad. I have much more down-time than you. So, perhaps all you need is a break. I don't know how it works for you at the Mossad, but why don't you tell Anna that you're taking a few weeks off? I'll do the same, and we can meet up somewhere far away from all of the stress and pressure. What do you think?"

Eli laughed. "I love the idea, but don't you think it would be very obvious to Anna that we've been sleeping together when we both ask to take a few weeks off at the same time? I'm thinking that will be a dead giveaway that we're breaking rule number two." He continued changing into his business suit and thought of an alternative plan. "Here's what we can do instead: You sign up for another mission and I'll go ahead and take two weeks off. You accomplish your mission quickly, but don't report it. I'll meet you and we can spend a few days together. What do you think about that plan?"

She smiled as she wrapped the burka around her head, "I think it's the best we can do under the circumstances. I'll let you know the location as soon as I receive my next mission. Let's hope it's some-place warm and beautiful!"

They gathered their gear into the suitcases Olivia had deposited into the building several days before. Then they did a final sweep to make sure they hadn't left anything behind.

"Ready?" Eli asked.

"Yes let's do this. I've already called for the car. I vetted our driver two days ago. He's one of us. However, just to be safe, let me get a look at the driver when the car arrives. If it's not him, I'll signal you and we'll take action."

The black Mercedes wove down the narrow street and stopped outside the door Eli and Olivia were standing behind. She cracked the door and peered out, trying to get a glimpse of the driver, but couldn't see through the tinted windows. So, she exited quickly, ran around the back of the car, came up to the driver's-side window, and rapped on it with her knuckles. She held the nine-millimeter pistol ready in her other hand. The dark window rolled down and she "sliced the pie" of the car's interior, taking in the driver's facial features and the contents of each section of the car.

The driver said, "Good evening, Ms. Berg. We must move quickly. I've picked up communications that the authorities know something is amiss. I fear your time here is up. What is it the Americans say?" He frowned in thought and then raised his eyebrows. "Ah, yes. You don't want to 'wear out your welcome.'"

Satisfied that everything was good with the driver, Olivia dropped the pistol into her purse and motioned for Eli to come out. The driver released the trunk lid and Eli deposited their suitcases, slammed the trunk closed, and then walked around the car and held the door open for Olivia. They drove in silence toward the airport for several minutes before Eli spoke. He said to the driver in perfect Arabic, "Peace be upon you, my brother. Thank you for the ride. What is your name?"

To Eli's astonishment, the driver answered in perfect Hebrew, "And peace to you, my brother. You're welcome. My name is Mustafa and I am happy to be helping you and your wife tonight."

Eli bristled and reached for his pistol because no one was supposed to know their cover details.

"Ah, I see your astonishment, but do not be afraid. I know of your disguises and of your cover story. Again, do not be frightened, for I am not just employed by you — I am one of you."

Olivia turned to Eli and said, "It's okay. Remember? I already told you that he's one of us. I guess you don't interact much with other members on your missions like I do."

Eli shook his head. "No, I rarely work with anyone in the region because of how good the Mossad intelligence is. Their distrust of the Arabs is extremely high, and always has been. We can thank the thousands of years of useless bloodshed between the Christians and Muslims for that distrust. So, anyway, the risk of exposing the Orion Society goes up exponentially with each additional person I work with that is a native to this area of the world."

Eli leaned forward and patted Mustafa on the shoulder as they rolled up to the small Learjet on the airport runway. "Sorry that I was so jumpy. It's been a long few days. Thank you again. And peace be with you and your family."

CHAPTER 2

Orion Society Regional Headquarters, Moscow, Russia.

Eli took the ring from his pocket and placed it on the table in front of him. It had been less than twenty-four hours since his encounter with the demon. The encounter still weighed heavily on his mind. It had been the first time he had felt terrified since he was a young child. He was glad to get rid of it and never wanted to see it or be near it again. He cast a furtive glance around the table, at the elders of the Orion Society.

"Where is Sergei?" Eli asked as his eyes lighted upon Anna Papalova, who sat at the head of the table.

Anna smiled and softly said, "Eli, he's gone. He passed away two days ago from a sudden heart attack."

Eli's eyes widened at the news. "He couldn't be saved?"

"No, it wasn't that. Sergei died in his own bed in the middle of the night. He lived alone, and his chef found him when he arrived for work the next morning. He had walked into Sergei's bedroom to ask him what he wanted for breakfast. There was nothing that we could do."

Eli tilted his head to the right and squinted. "Natural causes, or was he killed?"

"We are still investigating. Unfortunately, the chef called the authorities, so now we have to fight all of that red tape. We did check the secret cameras though. The only thing that was odd during the night was that one corner of his bedroom was unnaturally dark. Almost as if there was a shadow lurking there."

Eli thought about the implications of the shadow and then pointed at the ring. "Speaking of shadows. As requested, there is King Solomon's ring. I must tell you though, that the story associated with it is true. I put the ring on my finger, and a demon appeared. I tried to take the ring off, but it was stuck. The demon tempted me and even shape-shifted into a beautiful, naked woman. I asked God to deliver me, the ring fell off of my finger, and then the demon disappeared. I was scared to death!"

Anna chastised him, "My dear, that's why we tell all of our agents only to secure the target and return with it to one of our vault locations. Something you've heard hundreds of times, yet you still didn't listen. You are lucky to be alive, young man."

Eli said, "Yes, I know. And, I'm extremely grateful to be alive." He looked at the ring and cleared his throat. "Oh, there's more to the story. There's a clear, glass-like sarcophagus and you can see a perfectly preserved body. There are also many other items in the cavern that might be of interest to us. Anyway, after thinking about what the demon said, I think that the man in the sarcophagus might be Alexander the Great. Because, the demon said something like, 'You know, that Alexander guy wasn't so great.' So, I'm guessing you'll want to do a secret excavation."

"That's wonderful news, Eli! We'll put that mission in the queue and prioritize it. But now we have something else to discuss with you. Eli, your next mission is of utmost importance." She smiled. "As they all are, I know. However, what we've recently discovered in an interpretation of an ancient text is quite disturbing. We are still analyzing the text and its implications, but we know enough to realize that we're dealing with something that might destroy humanity." She gazed around the room at the other members of the Society before her eyes settled on Eli once again. "We voted and unanimously agreed that we must retrieve and protect the ancient object. Eli, the mission objective is to go back to Alexandria and steal an ancient chest from the museum. And then get it to Moscow safely so that we can secure it in our vaults. The details of how you achieve the mission, as always, are your decision. However, I think you'll be intrigued by the details of the story. Not everyone in the room has had the opportunity to read it, so I'll read it aloud for the benefit of everyone. It's a tale told by one of two assistants who were traveling with a British explorer and a Knight of Malta. After careful consideration, we believe that the story is true, or enough at least to warrant further inspection."

Anna began to read from the transcript of the text. "The year was fifteen thirty-four AD, and the location was the Valley of the Kings, near Luxor, Egypt.

Andre de Montbard, a renowned Knight of Malta, gazed upon the polished stone chest with both awe and envy. In awe of the beauty of the intricate carvings that covered the entire box. In envy of George Ashtor, a British explorer, the very man he was hired to protect on this hellish journey. They had arrived in Alexandria forty-four days before and had been wandering the desert for nearly forty days in search of the tomb in which they now stood. The journey had almost gotten all of them killed, and they were dangerously low on food and water, but the fool Ashtor was right after all. The entire structure was lined with a fortune in gold and precious gems.

Montbard was so tired he could barely move, but not only physically tired. He was tired of wealthy aristocrats like Ashtor, who seemed to be always interfering in the Knights' affairs. He questioned in his mind why the fool Ashtor should receive all of the riches. He knew that, as a Knight of Malta, it was his right to be wealthy!

Montbard considered the situation for a brief moment and quickly came to the conclusion that Ashtor must be killed. He decided that he would tell Ashtor's two assistants, who had been left outside as a safety measure in case they became trapped in the tomb, that Ashtor had tripped and fallen into one of the many spears jutting from the wall. It would be a shame that Ashtor had met such an unfortunate death. He would strike a deal with Ashtor's assistants to help him remove the treasure from the tomb and transport it back to the ship waiting in Alexandria. Once they had all the cargo loaded, he would then kill the two assistants, leaving absolutely no trace of what had truly happened. Montbard would return to Malta a hero, and the money would bring the Knights back from their impending demise and ensure their greatness.

Ashtor was too consumed with examining the stone chest to notice Montbard moving closer to him. He was trying to decipher the strange writing on the chest and leaned in for a closer look at precisely the moment Montbard swung his sword downward, narrowly missing Ashtor. His sword glanced off the chest.

"Ashtor spun and said, "What has come over you, man?"

Montbard didn't see a need for discussion, because he had already made his decision. The Knights of Malta would be restored to their full glory, and he would see to it this very night. He lunged again at Ashtor but stumbled over something unseen on the floor, and before he could fully regain his balance, Ashtor had struck him in the head with an ancient Egyptian canopic jar, which he had snatched quickly from beside the stone chest. The jar broke into pieces over Montbard's head, which dazed him as he fell to the floor, lost his grip on his sword, and watched with blurred vision as it clanked across the stone floor. He slumped to the floor of the tomb as dust from the long-deceased Egyptian pharaoh's disintegrated internal organs settled over his prone form.

"Ashtor quickly turned to leave the tomb and ask his two assistants to help him secure Montbard, then start hauling out the treasure. But, as Ashtor walked by, Montbard grabbed his ankle and pulled with all his strength, which sent Ashtor sprawling into the wall on the other side of the tomb. Montbard quickly rose to his feet and pulled his dagger from the leather sheath on his hip and ran at Ashtor, who was almost back on his feet. Montbard crashed into Ashtor at a full run, sending him hurtling back into the tomb's wall.

As Ashtor hit the wall, he reached for his dagger and feigned weakness by moaning and begging for Montbard to stop. Montbard placed his hand on Ashtor's shoulder and spun him around only to find that Ashtor had been bluffing: Ashtor drove his dagger deep into Montbard's shoulder. In a fit of rage over his mistake and in terrible pain, Montbard quickly raised his dagger and stabbed it directly into Ashtor's neck, hitting a major artery. He let Ashtor fall to the floor. Ashtor reached up and pulled the dagger from his neck, and a fountain of blood poured forth. He looked at Montbard with hate-filled eyes and struggled to get up and mount a counterattack. But instead, he fell back to the floor and took his last, haggard breath.

"'Montbard was covered in his own blood and the blood of George Ashtor. The coppery scent filled the small tomb as their blood saturated the fine layer of sand on the stone floor.

"'He breathed a sigh of relief. He had won the fight, and now stood silently for several seconds thinking about his plan before finally coming to the conclusion that Ashtor's dagger must be removed from his shoulder. So, he steeled himself for the inevitable pain, placed a hand around the hilt of the dagger, and pulled with all his might. The dagger slid out with a deep sucking noise. Removing the dagger caused the blood flow from his wound to become even heavier, which he knew from many years of fighting must be stopped immediately or he would die within hours from blood loss. He dreaded his only alternative, which was to cauterize the wound using one of the burning torches they had brought with them to light the tomb. He knew he had little time to waste, so he grabbed a torch, extinguished it on the wall and plunged the red-hot embers on the end of the torch into the wound on his shoulder. He ground it in deeply to make sure he cauterized the leaking blood vessels and cried out in agony, then bent over and vomited on the floor from the intense pain.

"'Montbard allowed himself a few minutes to regain his resolve and to re-collect his thoughts before he exited the tomb to kill Ashtor's assistants. Still in a daze, he determined that before he left the tomb to approach them, he had to investigate what it was on the stone chest that had captivated Ashtor's attention so profoundly. He turned toward the chest and took a step forward, but quickly became dizzy from the blood loss and pain, and ended up stumbling across the tomb, where he ran right into the stone chest. It teetered precariously on its base as Montbard reached out to steady it. His vision began to blur, and his hands missed the box entirely. It fell off the base and onto the floor of the tomb. He slid down the pedestal, slumping to the floor. With blurred vision, he noticed that the lid had come off the box and what appeared to be black sand had poured out of it.

"'Montbard glanced back at the pile of black sand near the golden box, but it didn't seem the same—it appeared more spread out now. As he stared at the sand, he shook his head vigorously to try to clear his vision, because the sand now seemed to be moving toward him. He sat there, mesmerized by the moving sand as it reached him and started to cover his hands and move up his arms. The black sand moved quickly to the dagger wound in his shoulder. At first, he felt a slight tingling sensation at the injury, but then the tingling became an intense pain as the tiny creatures burrowed their way inside of his body. Montbard screamed in agony as they began to replicate and destroy his body from the inside out. As he writhed in the final throes of death, he heard a voice *over and over in his head proclaiming, "I Am Atum." These words were spoken in his mind in English, French and many other languages he didn't understand.*

"'The tiny creatures destroyed every cell in Montbard's body, killing him within seconds. Their job complete, they worked their way back up to the surface of his body and exited out of his mouth, eyes, ears, and nose. They fell to the sandy floor of the tomb, moved back to the chest, and entered it. For a moment everything was still, then mysteriously the chest righted itself, and then the lid levitated above it and lowered itself down to seal the chest again. If anyone had been left alive in the tomb, they would have heard tiny locks engage to prevent the lid from opening. The beautiful chest and the small creatures inside resumed their wait until Atum would give them their next task or the internal timer on the box would allow the lid to be removed again. Only Atum knew when that time would come."

Anna laid the paper down on the table, removed her reading glasses, and stared at Eli.

"We don't know how much of the story is true. The way it was written is very strange to me. Sometimes it's as if Montbard himself was telling the tale, because how could an assistant know some of those things? For example, how could the assistant know what Montbard was saying or thinking? Perhaps they weren't waiting outside, but rather, inside the tomb and witnessed the entire event. However, that's not important because, like all of the things we are involved in, there's always some level of truth."

Anna looked at her notes and collected her thoughts, then said, "You'll be doing this mission alone. We've already deployed Olivia on another mission, and all other agents are engaged. Eli, we have reason to believe that the ancient chest described in the story may be what we might call today a doomsday device. So, it's imperative that it is retrieved and brought back here safely. Do you have any questions?"

Eli stared at the rich wood of the mahogany table and contemplated the implications of the story he had just been told, and, for a split second, doubted that there was any truth in the story. But then he remembered his encounter—anything was possible. He slowly shook his head, looked up at Anna, and said, "No questions, but I'm going to need some technical support on this. Is Nick Brown available?"

Anna nodded. "Yes, he's available in a support role only. He can send all of the pertinent information to your smart watch. Work with him on whatever you need. Good luck, Eli."

Eli nodded to the group and said, "Thank you. See you in a few days!" He scooted back from the table, stood, and walked out of the room to begin planning his next mission.

He had already booked a first-class ticket on the next flight to Alexandria by the time his feet hit the pavement outside of the museum. He sighed and muttered to himself as he hailed a taxi, "No rest for the wicked, I suppose. But at least I have time to pack a bag, and eat dinner before I have to board the plane." He pulled up the airline confirmation e-mail on his phone and laughed. His plane would be taking off in one hour and twenty-seven minutes. *Plenty of time!*

CHAPTER 3

Alexandria, Egypt

Eli disconnected the call with Nick Brown and smiled. The computer whiz had never failed him, nor ceased to amaze him. In fact, Nick already had most of the supplies delivered to the various locations where Eli would need them. Nick always swore that his computer helped him with planning simulations and that was how he knew exactly what to do. Eli wasn't big on technology and really didn't care how Nick did what he did. He merely appreciated that the fellow Orion Society member always came through for him.

He walked into the museum in Alexandria to get a tactile feel for the layout. The blueprints Nick provided were always accurate, but Eli liked to experience the location before he did the job. His eyes took in everything from the number of guards on duty to the type of security cameras that stared back at him from the ceiling. What he sought wasn't on the main floor anyway, but deep within the basement-level storage facilities. Disabling the security system would be an easy task for him. But the guards were a problem. There were just too many of them. He had counted fourteen so far, and he wondered if there would be more or fewer guards at night. He pretended to look at one of the many ancient Egyptian artifacts on display and reasoned to himself that in all previous thievery jobs he had done, there were always fewer at night.

He muttered under his breath, "You're overthinking it. Time to quit thinking and start doing."

He turned away from the display case and resumed his leisurely walk through the remainder of the museum. He mentally matched each doorway to the ones he had viewed on the blueprints. The one he had just walked by would take him to the basement levels. He made a mental note of its location and quickened his pace as he neared the exit doors. He left the museum and walked across the street, then through the front door of one of the most popular nightclubs in Alexandria. Nick Brown had delivered once again by securing him the room that adjoined the club's garage, which housed his getaway truck. Eli hadn't been to the room yet, so he didn't know what to expect, but Nick had come through for him on every other mission. So, Eli wasn't sure why he was nervous. Then it dawned on him, and he whispered between clenched teeth, "It's that fucking King Solomon's ring. Put it out of your head and focus, Eli!"

Eli walked through the club and waved at the bartender, who was restocking shelves with alcohol for the upcoming night's activities. He eyed the door at the end of the expansive dance floor and walked toward it, feeling in his pocket to locate the key. Eli unlocked the door and swung it open, revealing a long hallway with doors interspersed on either side. He walked to the rooms Nick had rented for him, unlocked the first door, and stepped inside the brightly lit room, smiling at the unopened crates covering the floor. He shut the door quietly behind him and walked over to the crates to begin prying the lids off with a crowbar. The crates contained the equipment he would need to bore the tunnel to the museum, and the miniature train tracks and a small electric pulley system that he would use to quickly traverse the distance to and from the museum. Nick had suggested that it would take two nights to complete the tunnel system. The noise from boring the tunnel would be minimal, but it was an unnecessary risk in the daytime, so the only alternative was to use the boring machine at night when the nightclub's loud music would provide the perfect cover. He looked at his watch and noted that it would soon be time for him to get to work. The club opened in forty-three minutes, and he knew that he had to make every hour count. He ran through a mental checklist of what needed to be done and then started assembling the small tunnel-boring machine. As he assembled it, he began to realize just how small the diameter of the tunnel would be. The tracks and the electric pulley system weren't just for speed. Nick had sent them because the tunnel wouldn't be large enough for him to crawl through unless he inched his way along on his stomach.

His watch vibrated, alerting him of an incoming encrypted call. He put his earpiece in and tapped the watch to accept the call.

"Cohen here, what's up, Nick?"

"Have you started boring yet?"

"No, but I'm assembling the tunnel-boring machine now. Why?"

"Good, because I forgot to tell you to set the boring machine to dig at an angle instead of straight down so you can lay the tracks for the electric car. Oh, and like I told you before, once you turn on the boring machine, it will take a few minutes to warm up. Wear your protective gear just in case there's a radiation leak, and it will also protect you from the heat. That's the best one of those I've ever built! It actually melts the rock to create the bore and then super cools it afterward. So, be careful. It has two business ends... One for extreme heat and one for extreme cold. Touching either end will cause tremendous damage to you. Any questions?"

Eli thought for a moment and tilted his head to the side as he envisioned an ancient tunnel beneath him.

"No, no questions for now. If I think of any, I'll reach out to you. The music in the club has begun, so I had better get started on the tunnel. Talk soon."

Eli disconnected the call and mumbled as he switched on the machine, "I need a vacation far away from my chosen occupation!"

Eli stood and rehearsed the theft again in his mind while he waited. It was one of his quirks. He obsessively thought of every detail of each mission nonstop until he completed it.

A soft beep broke him out of his thoughts, and he glanced at the boring machine. The lights glowed green, indicating that the technological marvel was ready for use. Eli slipped into the protective suit and gloves, then lowered the full face guard. He crawled onto the small wheeled cart behind the boring machine and depressed the start button. He watched in amazement as the machine began to melt a hole in the floor.

Eli angled the machine so that it would bore a gentle slope before he leveled it out and began to drill straight toward the museum. Sweat, caused by the intense heat, ran down his forehead and stung his eyes. Even with the insulated, protective suit on, the temperature was quickly becoming unbearable. He craned his neck upward and checked the LCD screen, noting that he still had over one hundred meters to travel. The timer showed that he had only been boring for thirteen minutes, and the estimated completion time was over eight hours. Now he understood why Nick had predicted two days to drill the tunnel to the museum. Eli relented to the fact that he would have to take frequent breaks or else risk severe dehydration and potentially heatstroke. Anger boiled within him when he realized how physically demanding the job was going to be. He put the machine in reverse and rode it back into the room, then removed the face shield, picked up the satellite phone, and dialed Nick.

Nick answered on the second ring. "What's up, Eli?"

"I'll tell you what's up, you little shit! That boring machine generates so much heat that it's unbearable to operate. That's what's up!"

"Calm down, Eli. Did you turn on your suit's chiller module that I sent with the boring machine?"

"I don't know anything about a chiller. All I know is that it's hotter than balls in here and I'm about to pass out!"

Nick snickered. "There's a small panel on the left wrist of the suit.

Open it. There are temperature and oxygen controls in there that you can use to manage your comfort levels. The machine also uses up all of the available oxygen because of the intense burn. The oxygen in the suit comes on automatically, but the temperature-control system doesn't, so battery power is conserved. I sent a spare battery pack with the suit, so keep one charging at all times so you won't have any downtime. Also, since you call me most of the time when I'm sleeping, I forgot to tell you something: I've already programmed the coordinates into the boring machine. It will guide itself to a maintenance closet inside the museum. You'll have to travel from there into the sub-basement levels where I'm betting you'll find the artifact you're looking for. Before you ask, let me explain. My calculations tell me that the sub-basement levels in that building are too fragile to have any disturbances to them. If we bored directly into those areas, the entire structure might collapse down on top of the sub-basement. Sorry about not telling you about the cooling system."

"No worries, Nick. Thanks for the help."

Eli turned on the chiller, and cool air immediately began to flow through the suit. He took Nick's advice and plugged in the spare battery pack to make sure it would be fully charged when he needed it, and then crawled back into the tunnel and started boring again.

The added comfort of the cool air circulating in the suit made the job bearable. So, Eli continued boring throughout the night, and finally slowed the boring-machine to a crawl, which made it operate almost silently. He was exhausted and hadn't slept in over twenty-four hours. But he desperately wanted to spend more time with Olivia, so he continued to stick with the plan he had devised earlier. If he pushed on, then he could shorten the mission by a day. He checked his watch, and it showed that he still had about nine hours of darkness left, which would give him enough time to complete the tunnel and take a quick nap before he began his mission. He was lost in thought when the tunnel-boring machine reversed course, and red lights started flashing. He shook himself out of his mild stupor and examined the LCD panel as the machine began to roll back through the smooth-walled tunnel. The LCD screen read, "Boring Completed." Only then did Eli relax and lay his forehead on the machine while he rode back to the nightclub's back room.

He heard the increased whine of the electric motor as it started up the slope, and he breathed an exhausted sigh of relief at the prospect of sleep. Too tired to get up, he merely rolled off the cart onto the floor, grabbed a nearby towel, and shoved it under his head to use as a makeshift pillow. Then he set his watch alarm to go off in four hours and lay there, playing the mission through multiple times in his mind. After several seconds, he blinked slowly while staring at the ceiling. Then fatigue overtook him, and he closed his eyes and entered a fitful sleep.

He dreamed of Olivia—a replay of the last time they had made love, their walks on the beach hand in hand, and staring into her ice-blue eyes. Then his dreams switched to the demon, as they had every night since the occurrence in Alexander the Great's tomb. The dream was different every time and felt very real. Tonight, the demon switched into the beautiful, nude woman, and he succumbed to her wiles. She straddled him and rode him hard. The pleasure he felt was beyond belief, and even though he knew what was happening, he didn't want it to stop. He focused harder and found the will to tell the demon to dismount, but it ignored him. Instead, its face transformed into Olivia's, and she leaned down and kissed him hard. He closed his eyes and melted into the kiss, moaning with pleasure. Then he remembered she couldn't be real and opened his eyes and pulled his mouth away. The hideous demon was only inches from his face and laughed mockingly at him, showing its double rows of teeth.

Eli bolted awake, screaming, "Nooooo!"

Sweat ran down his face, and his heart pounded. He scrambled up and ran for the door, but stopped short of turning the knob and exiting the room. He was filthy from head to toe from the tunnel-boring operation, and knew that he couldn't enter the bar because he would blow his cover. So, he turned, put his back against the door, and slid down to a seated position. He drew his knees up and wrapped his arms around them and wept openly for several minutes. His tears eventually dried up, as did the feeling of despair. He had a new feeling now. Anger. He had never felt this weak in his entire adult life. His Mossad training had instilled a mental toughness that had allowed him to always persevere in any situation, but not now. He was showing and feeling weakness, and it made him very angry.

He checked his watch and said to himself, "Get your shit together and keep it together, Eli!" He took a deep breath and exhaled slowly. "Fuck it, this mission is starting early. I need to get the hell out of this place as soon as possible!"

He stood and walked over to his duffel bags, unzipped them, and peered at their contents. He selected all-black clothing and boots in addition to black face paint and a black tactical baseball cap. Then he took a quick shower, dressed in his black clothing, and smeared the paint on his face.

After a final equipment check, he decided it was mission time. But, since he had fallen asleep earlier and hadn't assembled the tracks, he couldn't use the small train car. So, he improvised. He started the boring machine and turned it back toward the tunnel entrance. Then he lay down on the little cart and engaged the machine, beginning his journey back down to the other end of the tunnel. His alternative transportation worked flawlessly, and he brought the machine to a stop at the hole that led to the museum janitor's closet.

Eli crawled into the janitor's closet and removed his backpack. Then he proceeded to load up his two tranquilizer-dart guns to full capacity, hoping that he had brought along enough darts to subdue all of the guards in the museum if the need arose. He cracked the door and peered out, immediately noticing the small, red light on the security camera, which was aimed directly at him. He reacted immediately, quickly shutting the door and pulling out his secure satellite phone, then he dialed Nick Brown for assistance.

He waited impatiently while the phone rang for several seconds. A groggy voice answered, "Uh, hello? Nick here."

Eli laughed and said, "Sorry, Nick, I forgot about the time difference. Oh well, it really wouldn't have mattered anyway because I just started the mission and I've already hit a snag. I need your help with security because I can't get to the security room without being caught on camera. So, can you hack into their system and shut it down, please?"

Nick yawned and grumbled under his breath, "Fucking agents..."

"What's that?" Eli asked.

"I said, 'fucking agents.' You all keep me up at all hours of the night anymore."

Eli laughed quietly and said, "I'm glad to know we're so loved. Now, what about shutting down the security system? Can you do it?"

Nick snorted. "You're shitting me, right? You know who I am. Of course I can do it. Give me a minute, and I'll do even better than shutting it down. I'll leave the system up and feed fake video to the cameras so the guards won't suspect anything. Everything will appear perfectly normal to them.

Eli used the time while Nick was hacking the security system to check his dart guns to make sure they would function properly when he needed them. Then he pulled out his Sig Sauer pistol, ejected and reseated the magazine. He looked appreciatively at the gun and pulled the slide back, chambering a round, and slid the gun back into his shoulder holster.

Nick interrupted his routine and said, "There you go. All done. They won't see anything but the looping feed I noticed that they do a patrol rotation every thirty minutes. There are ten guards working tonight, and they patrol in pairs. So, you have six-minute windows to move around after the guards pass your location before the next pair shows up. That's theoretically anyway, as long as they don't change their routine. Good luck!"

Eli let out a slow breath and said, "Thanks, I've needed some luck lately."

He pulled the black ski mask over his face and cracked the door to the closet. Then he set his watch timer for six-minute intervals and waited for the guards to pass before he started the timer.

It only took a few minutes of waiting before a pair of guards passed his location. He turned on the timer and waited for thirty seconds before sliding through the door and gently closing it behind him. Playing his mental map of the museum in his head, he started walking through the administrative offices. He paused at the door that lead to the exhibits and nervously checked his timer again. Noting he still had plenty of time, he open the door and sprinted through the exhibits.

Eli spotted the basement stairwell door ahead to his right and veered for it, breaking into a slow jog. He glanced at his timer, which told him that he had more than sixty seconds left before the next guard rotation would walk through. He opened the door and flipped his night vision goggles down over his eyes, casting the stairwell in an eerie green hue. The walls were damp, and when he breathed in, he gagged on the musty smell. Not wanting to breathe the moldy air any longer than he had to, he set off down the stairs in search of the room that contained the small stone chest that he was supposed to steal. The only intelligence the Orion Society had on the chest was that it had been on display until recently. The museum curators had decided to refresh some of the exhibits, and they had removed it from the main floor and placed in the archives. Unfortunately, there wasn't any intelligence on which room it might be in, so he had to search all of them until he found it. He reached the first subfloor and picked the lock on the first room he came to, then entered it. There wasn't anything in the room except for maintenance supplies, so he quietly shut the door and went to the next one, repeating his lock-picking process. The second room was lined floor to ceiling with thick, wooden shelving and crates covered with dust. He looked down and noticed that the dust on the floor was also undisturbed, so he reasoned that what he was looking for wouldn't be in the room. He quietly closed the door and walked to the end of the long hallway, purposefully skipping the rooms in the middle. He broke into the last room and shined his flashlight around the room. What he saw was more of what he had found at the other end of the hallway, nothing bust dust-filled shelves. There were four floors to the basement level, so he chose to repeat his search process and keep descending until he found a room that had freshly disturbed dust.

He had been searching for over forty-five minutes and was starting to become concerned because, the longer he was in the museum, the higher his chance of being detected became.

He was working through the third basement level when his luck changed.

He shone his flashlight into the room, revealing freshly made footprints on the dusty floor.

"Jackpot," he whispered.

The footprints led deeper into the room and stopped at sets of metal shelving that lined the back wall. Four small, wooden crates looked newer than the others, and the dust on the shelving was disturbed where they sat.

Eli pulled the first crate off of the shelving and placed it on the floor, but almost dropped it. He hadn't expected a crate so small to be as heavy as it had been. He glanced at the crate and then his eyes began searching the room for something to open it with.

Not far away, there was a small bench with tools lying on it. Ideally, Eli preferred a crowbar, but there wasn't one, so he selected an ordinary claw hammer and a flathead screwdriver. Eli walked back to the crate and opened it. All he could see was what appeared to be straw or some type of packing material lining the top of the crate. He tentatively poked at it with the screwdriver and then reached down and shoveled out the packing material with his hands. The object in the crate was an Egyptian canopic jar, not the small chest he was looking for. So, he grabbed the next crate and repeated the opening process. This crate contained some small figures of the Egyptian god Horus. Eli checked his watch, noting the elapsed mission time, and shook his head. It was taking entirely too long, and his risk of being caught was skyrocketing by the minute. Frustrated but not deterred, he grabbed the next crate and repeated the process. This time there was a small chest in the crate, and his heart jumped, hoping that he had found what he was looking for and could complete the mission. He pulled the small chest out of the crate and carefully turned it in his hands, examining every detail. What he saw didn't match what had been described to him in the mission briefing, so he gently placed it back in the crate. Only two small crates remained on the shelving. He selected one, opened it, and removed the packing material. It was another small chest, and although more reserved this time, his pulse still quickened. He pulled it out and looked at it. It matched the description he had been given, but it was strangely warm in his hands. He frowned with concern at the small chest's warmth because he didn't want any more strange encounters, but his curiosity was too strong. He tugged on the lid to open it and see what the chest contained, but it wouldn't budge. So, he stuck the screwdriver in one of the corners of the lid and pried. That didn't work either, and he cursed at his bad luck but then said softly, "Remember that damned ring, Eli. Remember the ring. You don't know what's in the chest, and it's better that way. Complete the mission."

Self-talk session over, he packed the chest back into the crate and quietly nailed it shut. He picked it up and crept to the door, listening carefully. Not hearing anything, he cracked the door open and peered out. The hallway was clear, and so far, the mission hadn't hit any major snags. He vowed to not be so hard on Nick because the kid was amazing.

He ran to the stairs and started climbing them, but stopped cold in his tracks when a door opened above him and light shone into the dark stairwell. Caught between floors, he did the only thing he knew to do, which was to descend the stairs and enter the next floor he came to. He quietly closed the stairwell door, took a few paces down the hallway, and turned to face the stairwell. He set the crate down and pulled out one of his dart guns, then did the only other thing he could do: He tried to hail Nick on his smart watch, but couldn't get a signal. He needed to know the positions of the guards, and he needed that information now.

He jumped when the door opened, and a guard stepped through. The guard was even more startled, and fumbled with his radio while reaching for his taser. Eli was faster. He brought the dart gun to bear and shot the guard in the chest. The guard's eyes went wide in confusion, and he grabbed the dart and pulled it out. But it was too late. The dart had already delivered the drug into his body, and he began to wobble and then fell to the floor in a heap. Eli watched him drop and then turned his attention back to the crate. He picked it up again and turned to walk around the guard. Much to his horror, the guard had his radio to his lips. Eli dropped the crate and lunged for the guard's radio, but he was too late. The last thing the guard said was, "Help! Basement level three!"

Eli's time was up. He grabbed the crate and started running up the stairs two at a time because he knew that it was imperative that he make it to the main floor of the museum where things were more open. The basement levels were nothing more than a single hallway each, with rooms on one side. There would be nowhere to hide down here where he wouldn't eventually become trapped.

He stopped at the first-floor landing, put his ear against the door, and listened. He could hear voices, but they sounded distant, so he cracked the door and looked out. Nothing was in his immediate field of vision, so he took a considerable risk and threw the door completely open and sprinted out, back in the general direction of the janitor's closet. Sirens wailed in the distance and the voices of the guards, telling him to 'halt,' followed him as he ran.

Since he had been spotted by the guards, he knew that he couldn't go straight to the janitor's closet. He would have to lose them or disable them, and only then could he make his way to the tunnel and the safety of the bar across the street. He made a split-second decision to stand and fight, because evading them would take too long and give reinforcements time to arrive.

He bolted around a display, dropped the crate on the floor, and backed quickly down the aisle until he felt the wall touch his back. He pulled both dart guns from their holsters and aimed them at the edge of the display.

The first guard rounded the corner at a full run, and Eli efficiently shot him in the neck. The man skidded to a stop at his feet. The next guard ran up to the corner of the display and peeked around, but he was too slow. Eli shot him in the face, and he crumpled to the floor. The other guards saw their coworker go down and stopped short of the display, instead taking up protected positions behind chariots, statues, and various other Egyptian artifacts.

The sirens outside began to grow louder, and Eli knew he was already out of time. So, he decided to go on the offensive. He calmly walked around the display and started acquiring and eliminating targets. Most of the frightened guards didn't put up much of a fight, and Eli reasoned that there should only be around two left if he was counting correctly. But he had no idea where they were hiding. So, he tried a new tactic.

He said, "I won't harm you if you let me go peacefully. I don't want to hurt anyone, I simply want to leave."

He slowly stepped backward until he rounded the corner of the display he'd hidden behind only moments before. Then he turned to pick up the crate and felt electricity jolt through his body. He spasmed on the ground as a pair of boots appeared in front of his eyes, and then a yellow taser gun with wires sticking out of it. Then he felt a knee in his back, and one of his arms was pulled behind him. The guard reached for Eli's other arm, but Eli knew that he couldn't allow the guard to cuff him or he would definitely be captured, and that was not an option. He replayed his Mossad training in his mind in a split second, remembering all of the times he had been tased and the mental fortitude it took to shorten the period you were disabled. He focused his mind on his next move, and although he was still twitching and the pain in his muscles was tremendous, he pushed up with his free hand and squirmed free of the guard's knee. He grabbed the guard's foot and pulled with all of his strength. The guard fell to his side, and Eli was on him in the blink of an eye.

Eli said, "I told you that I didn't want to hurt you, but now you're starting to piss me off!"

He slapped both of the guard's ears simultaneously and then did a chop directly to both collarbones, breaking them instantly. The guard howled in pain as blood ran from his burst eardrums.

Eli stood and looked down at him. "You probably can't hear me, but I'm sorry. You were wasting too much of my time, and I really have to go. You'll be in pain for a few days, but otherwise, you'll be fine."

Eli's head spun toward the clanking sound of the metal gates that covered the main entrance. They were opening slowly. The reinforcements—most likely police—had arrived. He had no desire to spend any time in an Egyptian prison, so he stood, grabbed the taser wires, and ripped them from his back, wincing from the sharp pain. Then he grabbed the crate and sprinted for the janitor's closet.

He had just closed the door when he heard the pounding of footsteps and the yells of the reinforcements as they discovered the disabled guards. Not wasting another precious second, he climbed down the hole in the floor of the janitor's closet and rode the tunnel-boring machine back to his hideout behind the nightclub.

He slid off the sled and crossed the room, depositing the small crate into a backpack, then hurriedly cleaned the black grease from his face and dressed in street clothes. Then he reapplied his Arab makeup, wig, and brown contact lenses. His final act before leaving the room was to place incendiary devices on the tunneling machine and the other equipment he would leave behind. He set the timers, and in two minutes the evidence would be reduced to melted slag, leaving no trace of his presence. He had enacted the failsafe plan and, and unfortunately, the nightclub would burn to the ground as a result of his actions.

He skirted the edge of the nightclub, avoiding the bar and dance floor. The thumping music and flashing lights helped disguise his movements. He reached the front door but didn't exit. His last act was to pull the fire alarm and wait for the music to stop and the patrons to start exiting the club. When they had started filing out the door en masse, he blended in with them and walked out into the street.

Eli walked with the crowd for a while and then veered off onto a side street that led him to a car that had been prearranged for him by

Nick Brown. He unslung the backpack, opened the door, and climbed into the driver's seat. Then he reached over and felt around under the passenger-side floor mat. The key was right where Nick had told him it would be, and his opinion of the computer geek rose higher for the third time that night. He put the key in the ignition, started the car, and merged into traffic, taking a direct route to his safe house where he would stay for the remainder of the night. He stopped and left the car three streets over from the safe house, which was located in the busy heart of the city—a precaution that he always took after almost getting killed years earlier.

Eli blended in with the people on the streets and scanned for anything amiss that would be a telltale sign that the location wasn't safe. He passed the apartment building that contained the safe house, proceeded further down the busy street, and stopped at a food vendor. He purchased a kabob of grilled meat and strolled back to the apartment building. Satisfied that he wasn't in danger, he entered the building and made his way to the apartment on the third floor of the building. He paused outside the door, drew his silenced pistol, and entered the apartment. He slid the deadbolt lock into position and allowed his eyes to adjust to the dimly lit interior. The faint glow from the street below was the only thing illuminating the small, three-room apartment. He stepped forward and quickly cleared each room before he risked turning on a light. Then he took the backpack off and slumped onto the hard sofa, leaned his head back, and closed his eyes, replaying the night in his mind. He opened his eyes long enough to set his watch alarm for eight thirty the next morning, which would allow him almost two hours of precious sleep.

The mission had been a success but hadn't gone entirely according to plan. However, true to his self-appointed vow, no innocents had died tonight, and he took solace in that fact. The most unfortunate thing was that he'd had to use the sterilization backup plan and burn the evidence and the nightclub in the process. The owner would most likely take a financial loss, but that was an acceptable risk. He hoped everyone had made it to safety after he tripped the fire alarm.

Now, all he had told do to complete the mission was to pose as the pilot of a commercial aircraft and fly it to Moscow the following morning. He would hide the stone chest deep in a case of fine Egyptian cotton pajamas. He began to rehearse tomorrow morning's masquerade as a pilot in his mind when fatigue and sleep finally overtook him.

CHAPTER 4

Eli slipped into his latest disguise, a flight suit that had the Wear400 logo on it, a major Egyptian cotton manufacturer. He had already hidden the chest in one of the hundreds of boxes of pajamas that lined the cargo hold of the plane. Pajamas were one of Egypt's most significant exports in their ever-growing trade business with Russia, with several shipments flying to Moscow every week. Eli's disguise was great. This was another one of Nick Brown's ideas. Eli didn't know how Nick had pulled it off, but he had arranged for Eli to pilot one of the cargo jets. Admittedly, he was slightly nervous at the prospect of flying the massive plane because he only had simulation training on it. The majority of his actual flight time was on smaller jet aircraft.

He muttered and began his self-talk habit: "Come on. You've been in worse situations than this. I mean, the worst thing that can happen is that you'll crash the damn thing and die. You're certainly not going to get caught. This is the best mission departure setup you've ever had! Shake it off!"

Eli laughed nervously and rolled his head around in an attempt to relieve some of the muscle tension and exhaustion that plagued him, thanks to the tunnel-boring machine. He closed his eyes and took a deep breath, then opened them and began his ground inspection of the aircraft before boarding it. Satisfied that the plane was airworthy, he climbed in and settled into the captain's chair. The copilot was already onboard and offered a gruff greeting. Then the man's eyes squinted in suspicion as he turned to Eli and said, "I don't know you. Where's Amir? He usually pilots this flight, and I've been flying with him for years."

Eli glanced over and said, "He's sick today. I'm filling in for him. My name is Ahmed, what's your name?"

"My name is shut the fuck up. I ask the questions here. You answer them. Understand?"

Angered, Eli began to reply, but the man laughed, slapped him on the shoulder, and said, "Relax, I was just kidding. My name is Amit. Sorry, I couldn't resist!"

Eli quelled his anger and briefly joined in the laughter, but then his thoughts went back to how he had never flown that particular aircraft, nor was he familiar with air traffic patterns in Egypt. He turned to Amit and said, "So, now back to business. I'm not from this area, so I'd rather have you at the controls for takeoff. You'll know the air traffic patterns and the air traffic controllers better. Do you mind doing that?"

Amit smiled. "No, I don't mind. Amir and I take turns taking off and landing all of the time."

They made it through their preflight check with no issues and taxied onto the runway. Amit applied the throttle, and they hurtled down the runway and lifted into the clear blue skies surrounding Alexandria.

Amit glanced over and said, "The flight time to Moscow is about four hours. We usually split the flight between ourselves. Whoever takes off gets the first shift while the other person naps. Then, at the halfway point I wake you up, and it's your turn to stay awake and make sure we don't crash. Sound good?"

Playing his role perfectly, Eli nodded and said, "That's the best thing I've heard all morning. I'm exhausted." He looked down, set his watch alarm to go off in two hours, and closed his eyes. But it took him well over an hour and a half to go to sleep. Every time he would doze off, his eyes would snap wide open, his heart racing from dreams of the demon.

Amit turned to Eli, eyebrows raised, and said, "Are you okay, Ahmed? Bad dreams, perhaps?"

Eli answered between gasping breaths, "Yeah, something like that. I haven't slept for more than fifteen minutes uninterrupted in the last few days." Eli smiled and wagged his finger. "But I'm going to keep trying to get my share of the rest. So, don't think you're going to get more than your two hours."

Amit shook his head and said, "I would never dream of it. Pun intended." Then he chuckled at his own joke.

Eli sighed and slumped back into his seat, resting his head on his wadded-up jacket. He took a deep shuddering breath and closed his eyes.

Amit waited ten minutes after Eli's last movement and switched on the autopilot. He couldn't wait any longer, because any minute now, Eli's phone alarm would start blaring. So, he pulled a satellite phone from his pants pocket and texted a message to his counterpart in Moscow. "Confirmed. The Orion Society agent is sitting right next to me. So, there must be something of value in the cargo. Meet me at the Moscow airport."

He looked over at Eli, fast asleep, and thought of slitting his throat, but changed his mind because he needed Eli to lead him to whatever he was stealing from Egypt. Amit stared out the window, wondering what Eli could possibly be trying to deliver to Moscow. Whatever it was, it was important enough that he'd been taken off his mission and re-tasked with this one. His thoughts were interrupted by Eli's alarm blaring over the sounds of the cockpit.

Eli stretched and yawned. "Okay, it's your turn. Enjoy your rest, Amit."

Amit nodded and laid his head up against the side of the cockpit, using a folded blanket as a pillow.

The plane was still on autopilot, so Eli did a cursory check to make sure that they were still on target and flying at the correct altitude for their flight plan. Satisfied that they weren't going to crash if he took his eyes off the instruments, he dug into his pocket and pulled out a small notebook. He jotted down how many times he had dreamt of the demon during his short naps. He had been recording this data for two days and was determined to find a pattern in the dreams because he didn't think that they would stop until he did. And he desperately needed them to stop. The lack of sleep was starting to exhaust him severely. He stayed lost in thought for the remainder of the flight, until he heard a soft chime and the plane began to bank on its own. He checked their coordinates and realized that they were starting their approach to the Moscow airport. Still nervous, but determined to figure the plane out, he scanned the switches and dials until he found what he was looking for. He turned off the autopilot, adjusted the flaps, and lowered the landing gear as he lined up with the runway. He bled off speed and slowly descended toward the airport, speaking with air traffic control in fluent Russian. Eli brought the plane down hard and firmly pressed the brakes with his feet as he reversed thrust on the engines.

Amit woke with a shout and grabbed the controls before he realized that they were taxing down the runway. He said, "Remind me to never fly with you again. Your landing was horrible! I thought we had crashed!"

Eli laughed and said, "Well, we didn't, and you're still alive, so how about you shut the fuck up this time?"

"Very clever," Amit said and laughed heartily.

Eli taxied the plane to a cargo area on the tarmac, and they completed the power-down sequence. Then Eli extended a hand to Amit and said, "This is the end of the line for me. I won't be making the return trip to Egypt. In addition to being a pilot, I'm also a delivery boy on this job. I have to deliver a box of fine Egyptian cotton pajamas to President Sokolov. Anyway, it was nice to meet you, Amit. I wish you all the best."

Amit took Eli's offered hand and shook it furiously. "The sentiment is the same. Best of luck to you. Who will be the pilot on the return trip? No one told me of this."

Eli shrugged and said, "Sorry, I wish I could help, but I have no idea. They don't tell me anything, other than where to show up to ferry planes around the world."

Amit and Eli left the plane and walked in separate directions. Amit turned and watched Eli so he wouldn't lose track of him, and then he selected a spot where he could observe the unloading of the plane without being seen.

Eli went into the small building and used the restroom facilities. He splashed cold water on his face to try and combat the fatigue that he felt down to his bones. Feeling somewhat refreshed, he exited the restroom and walked slowly over to a rental van that had the keys lying on the middle console. He started the van and turned it around so that he could watch the unloading of the plane. Eli squirmed as he sat impatiently and watched for the box on which he had drawn a huge "X" on all sides. He had already instructed the ground crew to notify him when they brought the box out of the cargo hold, but he was too wired to wait for it. They were moving entirely too slowly, in his opinion. He laughed out loud and chastised himself, "You know what Grandpa used to say about opinions. They're like assholes. Everybody has one." He chuckled again and settled in for the wait. Luckily, he only had to wait a few more minutes before he saw the box with the "X" marks being unloaded.

He started the van and sped to meet the tow-motor driver. Eli hopped out of the van and opened the side door, directing the tow-motor driver to deposit the box inside of the van. He was shutting the side doors when he heard, "Eli, can I catch a ride?"

It was Amit, who was running to meet him. Amit slowed to a jog as he approached Eli and said, "There was a mix-up with my rental, and I figured if you're delivering to the President's house, then you'll go right by the National Hotel, which is where I'm staying tonight. Do you mind?"

Eli smiled and said, "No problem! I'm happy to help!"

Amit settled into the passenger seat, and Eli drove the van through an access gate to exit the airport facilities and pull onto the A-105 toward Moscow.

Eli glanced over at Amit and said, "Feel free to nap. We have about an hour's drive before we'll be near your hotel."

Amit said, "I can't sleep. It must be all of that coffee I drank after we landed. I really need to piss." He pointed at a Tatneft fuel station up ahead on the right. "Do you mind if we stop there?"

"No problem," Eli said.

Amit hopped out of the van and walked into the station, leaving Eli with the idling van. Amit walked into the restroom and relieved himself. He was washing his hands when another man walked up beside him and slipped a small pistol into his pocket. Amit looked into the mirror that reflected the man's face and nodded. The other man replied with a barely perceptible tilt of his head, then turned and left the restroom. Amit checked to make sure he was alone and then walked into one of the stalls. He pulled the pistol from his pocket and ejected the magazine, reseated it, and chambered a round.

Then he walked up to the passenger door of the van and opened it, pointing the pistol at Eli.

"Get out of the van and unlock the back. It's time to see what you've stolen."

It wasn't the first time that Eli had been held at gunpoint. He said, "Oh, shit. Really? You're with the Egyptian government?"

"No, my soon-to-be dead friend. I am most assuredly not with the Egyptian government."

"I'd really prefer to live. So, if not the Egyptian government, then who are you with?"

Amit frowned and said, "That's not important. What is most important right now is that you open up the back of the van. Do it!"

"Okay, okay. I'm going to open my door and get out. Then, I'll walk around and unlock the back doors."

Amit waved the gun for him to proceed.

Eli opened the door and jumped down. As soon as he was out of Amit's sight, he fell to the ground and rolled under the van, watching Amit's feet walk quickly to the back, then to the driver's side of the van. Eli shuffled in his direction, then reached out and grabbed both of Amit's ankles and pulled with all his strength. Amit fell backward, and a shot rang out. Eli scrambled out from beneath the van and pinned Amit's pistol hand to the ground. He gave Amit a quick open-palm nose strike, hoping to drive the cartilage into his brain. However, the angle was wrong, and there wasn't enough force behind the blow. Amit cried out in pain, but fought harder than before, ramming his knee into Eli's groin. Fighting nausea, Eli brought his right forearm across Amit's throat and leaned forward to add more of his body weight.

"Fucking Jew," Amit croaked before his eyes rolled back in his head and he took his final breath.

Eli reached for the pistol and struggled to stand. He stood bent over, trying to catch his breath, when he heard hushed voices. He looked up to find several people standing around.

He ran back to the van and squealed out of the parking area, continuing his journey north to Moscow before they could shut the road down hoping to intercept him. Knowing that his identity had possibly been compromised, he tapped on his smart watch to raise Nick Brown.

A few rings later Nick answered. "What's up Eli?"

"Nick, I hit a snag on the way to Moscow. Let's just say there's a dead guy and several witnesses. I'm probably also on camera, since it happened at a Tatneft fuel station. I need you to do some cleanup work, if you don't mind. At least get rid of the camera recordings. We can't do much about the people. Listen, I also need another form of transportation immediately. They're probably already looking for this van."

Nick said, "No problem. I'll take care of the recordings and inject some confusing information into the police systems. As far as transportation, the best I can do is to tell you that there is a grouping of restaurants and more fuel stations coming up in three point four kilometers, on your left. You'll have to get your own ride there. Do whatever you need to without worry. I'll take care of those cameras too. Good luck!"

Eli said, "Thanks, Nick," and tapped his watch to disconnect the call.

He had no problem stealing a ride. Regardless of the situation, he loved the challenge of breaking into cars. There were only two agents in the Mossad that were better at it than him, and he took pride in his skill.

His good mood was short-lived. The small crate in the seat beside him was emitting so much heat that he had to crack the windows on the car, and he wondered if he was being exposed to radiation. He increased his speed, risking getting pulled over by the police, but he no longer cared. He wanted to be away from the stone chest as much as he'd wanted to be away from King Solomon's ring. The last two missions were unlike any he had ever done before, and they both unnerved him.

He let out a grateful breath he had been holding when he entered the parking garage of the museum. The mission was finally over. Jonas, one of the Orion Society's guards, met him in the garage with a small cart.

Eli said, "Good evening, Jonas. How have you been?" Eli gladly deposited the crate on the cart.

Jonas frowned and said, "Well, Mr. Cohen, I was doing just fine until you brought whatever it is that's in that crate. I can feel the heat coming off of it from here! Are you sure it's safe to take into head-quarters?"

Eli rubbed his chin in thought.

"Well, it should be fine as long as you put it in a high-contain-ment vault. I honestly have only seen the outside of the chest. It wouldn't open, so I couldn't verify the contents. But if it contains what I was briefed on, it's very dangerous."

Jonas nodded and said, "Okay, that's what I'll do, and I'll notify the elders of the potential risk as well. Have a good evening, Mr. Cohen."

Jonas turned and pushed the cart toward the elevator, and Eli climbed back behind the wheel of the vehicle. He moved it to a section of the garage where the spaces were striped in purple, desig-nating that the car should be destroyed.

He didn't want to risk walking through the museum because he might be delayed by having to stop and talk to someone. He was exhausted and getting irritable. So, he walked up the ramp toward the street and swiped his keycard over the reader. The metal gate rose, and he stepped under it onto the sidewalk. Minutes later, Eli descended into the Moscow Metro, where he would catch a train to his apartment. He glanced at his watch as he waited for the train. It read 2:53 a.m. He had a mission debriefing with the elders in less than five hours.

CHAPTER 5

Orion Society Regional Headquarters, Moscow, Russia.

Eli walked into the State Historical Museum, a facade for the Orion Society headquarters in Moscow. It had only been three days since he had last sat at the big mahogany table, but this time there were more elders present. Only one chair was available at the table, and Anna motioned for him to sit in it. Whatever they had been discussing before he entered the room must have been very important because the tension hung in the air above the table like a dark storm cloud.

He cleared his throat, swallowed, and turned to Anna. "I've been thinking about taking a little time off if that's okay with you. The last two missions have taken a lot out of me mentally, and I really need to relax for a few weeks and recharge. The whole King Solomon's–ring incident with the demon still has me extremely shaken, and I can't quit thinking about it. I never believed in that stuff before, but it was very real, and it's changing the way I think about things tremendously." He started speaking faster as nervous energy flowed through him. "I'll do double missions or take some of the crap work when I get back. Whatever needs to be done. I just really, really need this right now."

Silence hung in the air for several seconds before Anna spoke. "Eli, I think we can accommodate your request, but I want to know about your most recent mission first. Jonas had just informed me before you walked into the conference room that you delivered the artifact and he has secured it in one of the high-risk vaults. Thank you for securing it. I have a feeling that it is one of the more dangerous things we have at this facility." She paused and stared up at the ornate conference room ceiling as if in deep thought and then quietly said, "Although there are some much more dangerous things in our other vaults around the world."

She paused again, then cleared her throat and continued, "I've also been watching the news reports, and I am relieved to know that no innocent people were killed during our operation. It would appear that we have a leak that needs to be plugged. The Thule Alliance is also after the chest, based on the difficulties you encountered after you landed in Moscow. We believe the man posing as your copilot works for them. The real question is: How did they know you'd be posing as a cargo pilot? That's one of the most obscure things I can think of. It's not like you were walking undisguised through the airport to catch a commercial flight. I can see how they might be monitoring places like that for our agents, but this man knew too much. I already have Nick working on finding the leak."

Eli shrugged and said, "Yeah, that's another reason I need some time off. I was with someone who could have killed me at any second. To make the pilot ruse work, I actually took my turn napping, and so did he, for that matter. I'm getting sloppy."

Eli shook his head, agitated. "But that's beside the point. The point is, the only reason he didn't kill me in the cockpit was that he didn't know what I was smuggling. The entire mission was cursed. A lot of things could have gone better, but it's done, and it was still successful regardless of the obstacles. There's nothing I could tell you about the mission that you don't already know."

He shuddered as a cold chill passed through his body. "I learned my lesson with King Solomon's ring and stopped myself from opening the chest. But there's something weird about the chest too.

Several times when I was handling it, it became very warm, and on occasion I swear I could feel something moving in it."

Eli raised his eyebrows and said, "So, the mission was completed successfully. How about that time off?" He smiled at Anna and nodded at the other Society members seated around the table.

She looked up and said, "Yes, of course, you certainly deserve it. Enjoy yourself!"

CHAPTER 6

Moscow, Russia.

Maxim Federov shifted in his seat and let out a deep sigh as the Russian Orthodox priest droned on. *"Where is the pleasure in life which is unmixed with sorrow? Where the glory which on earth has stood firm and unchanged? All things are weaker than shadow, all more elusive than dreams; comes one fell stroke, and Death in turn, prevails over all these vanities. Wherefore in the..."*

He wished the priest would hurry up and finish. He attended the funeral to keep up appearances, nothing else. Certainly, not to mourn his dead father. Federov was too calloused to feel love for anyone. He snorted lightly as he thought about his father. He hadn't seen him in several years, especially after he sold his companies and went to work for a museum. *A fucking museum! What an idiot!* The only thing that he was good for was his money. His father had made billions of dollars in the natural gas mining industry when Federov was a young boy. As an adult, Federov had taken some of that money and started his own business ventures, some legit, most not. Those ventures had made him a very young, forty-four-year-old billionaire, and the head of the largest crime syndicate in Russia.

He muttered under his breath. "Fuck it!" Then, he stood, pulled his phone from his pocket and dialed a number, bringing the phone up to his ear. Then, he proceeded to walk down the long aisle, the priest droning in the background. He was still walking down the aisle toward the exit when his call connected. "Dmitry, Federov here. Give me the status on the shipment? How many people did we harvest this week? Oh, and don't settle for anything less than twenty thousand for each of the young girls."

Dmitry cringed. He knew that he'd always work for Federov because the alternative was a bullet to the brain. He could stomach everything but the human trafficking. Federov had put him in charge of that part of the business a few weeks ago.

"Yes, sir. No less than twenty thousand for the girls. We harvested three boys and six girls from the streets last night. That's four over our average of five, so it was a good night, sir.

Federov smiled. He had chosen wisely to put Dmitry in charge of this part of the business. "Excellent! Let me know our totals as soon as all sales are final tonight."

Federov disconnected the call and dialed another number to check on other parts of his business. He walked up to his car, the chauffer opened his door, and he ducked inside.

He held the phone away from his ear. "Take me home, Anatoly."

He put the phone back up to his ear and continued his conversation, cursing the man on the other end of the call for his ineptness.

Then, he dialed Dmitry again.

"Yes, Mr. Federov"

"Dmitry, bring the prettiest girl to my house in the Khamovniki district. I'll be staying there tonight."

Federov chuckled and said, "I want to sample the product before it's sold tonight. I'll be there within thirty minutes. I have a business call to make when I get home, then I'll be ready for my sample."

"Yes, sir. I'll do it immediately!"

Federov busied himself for the duration of the ride to his house by checking in with his top business managers. He was wondering what the girl would look like when Anatoly pulled the car into the fourth bay of the attached garage. Federov was out of the car and bounding up the steps before Anatoly had shut off the engine.

Federov walked into his office and sat heavily into a plush, leather executive chair. He turned on his computer monitor and stared at the information, then smiled and stared off in the distance as his mind whirled.

Federov had made his decision. He peered at the computer screen one more time to admire the beautiful scientist. Dr. Lauren Martinez was a highly qualified physicist and medical doctor. He surmised, if anyone could create something that would give him immortality it would be her. He figured that he would need at least several hundred more years of life to complete his conquest to become the most powerful man in the world.

Federov picked up his mobile phone, looked at his computer screen, and typed her number into his phone. Then, he waited impatiently as the overseas call connected, drumming his fingers on the rich mahogany desk he sat behind.

He was greeted with voicemail, "Hello, you've reached Lauren Martinez. I can't take your call right now, so please leave a message."

He pressed the end button and screamed in frustration. "Fucking voicemail! Does this bitch know who I am?"

He hit redial and waited as his anger continued to rise.

After several rings his phone clicked in his ear and he was greeted by the same pleasant voice he'd heard on the voicemail message only seconds ago. "Hello? This is Lauren."

He quickly quelled his anger and did his best to sound as gentle and soothing as possible. He needed her to feel that he was a gentleman, and would be an excellent employer. He needed her to come work for him, and he needed it yesterday. There wasn't anyone else that had her specific credentials and skills.

"Dr. Martinez, my name is Maxim Federov and I have a proposal that I think you'd like to hear. I'm familiar with your research and all of the projects you've been involved in. The paper you compiled on the benefits of nano-technology in the human body is amazing!"

Lauren interrupted, "Thank you, but I'm not interested in doing any interviews right now. Have a nice day!"

Federov said, "Wait! Don't hang up. I want you to come work for me in nano-technology. Dr. Martinez, are you still there?"

Lauren was intrigued and paused before saying, "Yes, I'm still here, and I'm listening. Please continue. Tell me more about the work."

Federov cleared his throat and said, "Well, it's going to be quite interesting. Some of it has already started, but my scientists haven't made much progress. I will bring you on as Chief Scientist. The entire lab would report to you. To be frank, Ms. Martinez, I want to live forever, and I think nano-technology can give me that. Like I said, I know what you've accomplished in that field already, and I believe that you're the only person currently in the world who has a chance at succeeding. You'll have the best labs, equipment, and assistants that money can buy. I've spared no expense. I'll also pay you a five hundred thousand dollar signing bonus, one million dollars per year in salary, and a ten-million-dollar bonus when you're successful. Are you interested yet?"

A rivulet of sweat ran down Lauren's back as she stood in the small kitchen of the military base housing that she and Jack had shared over the past year. What she had just heard was a perfect description of her dream job. She brought her other hand to her forearm and pinched herself to make sure the moment was real.

She took a deep, shuddering breath and said, "Mr. Federov, uh, my research hasn't ever had a goal of achieving immortality. It has always been focused on assisting the natural healing mechanism in mammals and fish. So, there aren't any guarantees that I could achieve immortality, but I'll admit that it's possible. And, to be perfectly honest with you, that scares the living shit out of me!"

Lauren paused as guilt overtook her thoughts. She'd had thoughts of going back to work, but what about her relationship with Jack? Who was she kidding? He was never here, so there wasn't a relationship! But still, she loved him, and she knew that he loved her. The problem was their careers. He was a Delta Force Master Sergeant and was always gone on missions. Her passion for science and medicine had driven her since she was in college. When she had agreed to live on base with Jack, she had done it out of love for him. But she was going crazy living the military life. She was only happy when Jack was with her, and that was rare anymore.

Federov interrupted her thoughts. "Dr. Martinez, are you still there?"

She stammered, "Uh, yes, I'm still here. Sorry, I was considering your offer. I need more time to make my decision, but let me say this. I'm willing to fly to Moscow to meet with you, take a tour of the lab, and meet the existing staff. Then, I can make a decision. That's the best I can do right now, Mr. Federov."

Federov pumped his fist in the air. "Dr. Martinez, I'll arrange a private jet for you. Where are you currently located?"

"I'm in Fort Bragg, North Carolina. The closest city is Fayetteville, North Carolina."

Federov jotted down her location. "There will be a private jet at the Fayetteville airport for you by 8:00am tomorrow morning. I look forward to meeting you, Dr. Martinez."

Lauren's eyes widened. "Okay, that's a bit rushed, but I think I can make it. I have a few loose ends to tie up here before I can leave. Where will I be flying to?"

Federov answered, "Moscow my dear. See you tomorrow." Then he disconnected the call.

Lauren stood there dumbfounded. The opportunity of a lifetime had literally just fallen out of the sky right into her lap. She blinked slowly and brushed her long, dark brown hair out of her face. She blinked slowly again, but this time tears rolled down her cheeks. She retrieved a notebook and pen and sat down at the kitchen table and started writing her goodbye letter to Jack.

Dear Jack,

Jack, I love you, but you're never here, and I'm always stuck here by myself. Living in military base housing and hanging out with other mili-

tary wives and girlfriends isn't working out. They have their game nights, some of them have kids, and that's all well and good, for them. It's not me Jack. I'm not a housewife for sure, because we're not married, but for lack of a better word, I'm not a house-girlfriend either. Jack, we've talked about it before, many times, but nothing ever changes. You're not willing to give up the military, and even though I've temporarily given up my career to be with you, I'm literally dying on the vine pretending to be something I'm not. I'm not cut out for this. I'm not the person to stay behind, alone, for weeks at a time while you're deployed, which is always! I've have two degrees that I'm not using. A PhD in Physics and a Medical Doctor degree! How many times have I told you about all of the research projects I've been involved in prior to meeting you? I gave up my last job because I love you and I thought I could make this work! I think we might have been close to a cure for cancer, and I let it all go for the hope of a perfect relationship! I need to be doing something that I feel is worthwhile, Jack. Playing cards with other military girlfriends and wives doesn't fulfill me. My work does. Work that I've given up the past year so I could try to make us work. You have no idea how hard I've tried.

I have a job offer to lead a research team, and the possibilities of the good we can do is endless. I've agreed to meet with the owner of the company to discuss the offer. I'm flying out tomorrow for Moscow. I don't know when I'll be back. Please do know that I love you with all my heart, but I have to do this. I know that I could have called you on your satellite phone, but I just don't have the courage to do it. I'm afraid if I hear your voice, then I won't follow through with checking out this opportunity. Please forgive me.

Love Always,

Lauren"

She laid the pen down and her hands started to tremble. Then the tears began to flow again. But, took a deep breath and stood shakily. Then, she went to their bedroom, laid a suitcase on the bed, and started packing.

EPILOGUE

Eli thanked the elders, turned, and left the meeting room. Anna looked at the elders seated around her. "Eli has made tremendous progress, and I have high hopes for him. I believe he will do well in the Orion Society and play a key role in the future. But, in the meantime, we, unfortunately, have an open position to fill. Sergei's untimely death has been a blow to all of us, and I assure you, a tremendous blow to me. I've always been prepared to do whatever I can for our cause, but I never dreamt that I would be leading it. I pray that I can lead as well as he did." She looked around at the old faces and sighed deeply. "I've been thinking long and hard about something that I need to discuss with you and put on the table for a vote."

She cleared her throat and took a sip of water before continuing, "I think we should offer the seat to Sergei's only son, Maxim. His biggest positive attribute is that he clearly knows how to run a business. After all, he's a multibillionaire. I hear that his biggest negative, although I've never met him personally, is that he can be a bit shallow. But, under our tutelage, I think he could become a productive member of the Orion Society."

Hans Lieberman looked around the table with raised eyebrows

and said, "I didn't know Sergei had a son. I've been in this group for twenty-four years. He was never married. Is it the child of a whore?"

Anna waved dismissively at him. She chuckled and said, "Hans, you old fool, quit trying to get everyone riled up. We all know that you want your eldest son to be considered for the vacant seat. He will be interviewed like the others. I'm simply suggesting that we give Maxim the opportunity as well. I want to bring him in for an interview with us. Let's take the vote. All in favor?"

All the elders raised their hands, except for Hans.

Dmitry led the trembling girl in through the back entrance of Federov's house into the kitchen. Discretion was one of the top rules when working for Federov, and his employees paid with their lives if they didn't pay heed to that rule. But, Dmitry was also being discreet because he didn't want anyone to see him forcibly escorting a teenage girl around. Tears dripped from the girl's chin, and she had started to whimper, no doubt guessing this was her final destination for the night, and nothing good was going to come of it.

Dmitry admitted that he was a bad man. But not on the same level that Federov was a bad man. Dmitry had limits, and raping young girls was definitely one of them. His thoughts turned to visions of killing Federov, but he quickly dismissed the notion because then the money would end. His family depended on that money and he had debts to repay.

He called out loudly. "Mr. Federov, I'm here with the girl." He waited for a response, but heard nothing.

He glanced around the kitchen and his eyes settled on the various knifes sticking out of the knife block. He glanced over at the girl. She was eyeing the knives too.

He said, "Don't even think about it. If you make a move for those knives, I'll be forced to kill you. Please don't make me do that."

He stood there staring at the crying girl until a single tear rolled down his cheek.

He checked to make sure Federov wasn't nearby and then whispered, "Be quiet and don't move. I want to help you."

He walked over and selected a small paring knife, returned to where she stood, and slipped it into her coat pocket. "Now, you have a chance child. But, you are on your own."

Federov's voice boomed from the top of the main staircase. "Dmitry, is that you?"

"Yes, Mr. Federov. Shall I bring the girl up?"

"You're late! So, yes you fucking idiot, bring her up!"

Dmitry looked at his watch, baffled by how Federov thought he was late. He shook his head and escorted the girl up the servant staircase in the kitchen.

He delivered the girl to Federov's bedroom, shut and locked the door, and then turned to leave, bile rising in his throat.

Dmitry got in his car and stared blankly out the windshield as darkness quickly approached. He sat there for several minutes, tears rolling down his cheeks. He put his hand on the door latch several times, almost going back into the house to save the girl. Instead, he started the car, went to the nearest pub, and drank until he blacked out.

Federov was walking toward his bedroom when his phone rang. He answered angrily. "Yes, what is it?"

In Moscow, Anna raised an eyebrow and glanced at the Orion Society members seated around her. "Mr. Federov, this is Anna Pavlova. I have some business to speak about with you. It's about your father's estate. Can you meet with me tomorrow at three o'clock in the afternoon at the State Historical Museum?"

Federov frowned and shook his head. "I really don't have time for charities and antique donations, if that's what the meeting is about."

Anna said, "No, Mr. Federov, it has nothing to do with any of that. In fact, I can't disclose any details over the phone, but I know you'll be very intrigued to hear what I have to say. So, how about tomorrow at three o'clock?"

Federov grumbled, "I'll see what I can do." He disconnected the call and punched in the code on his bedroom door and stepped into the room. He grinned with anticipation when he saw the young girl sitting on the corner of his bed.

Deep beneath the Orion Society's Moscow headquarters, the stone chest glowed brightly, casting an orange hue on the walls of the vault. Then the glow slowly faded and the four tiny locks that secured the lid clicked open...

Join me for the rest of this fast-paced journey! Is Federov really as evil as he seems? What will happen to Eli and Olivia? Does Lauren take the job with Federov? And, what's in the mysterious stone chest?

Click or touch here to get AWAKENING, the first book in the Ancient Purge series, and continue the saga.
http://mcbassauthor.com/awakening-amazon

BOOKS IN THE ANCIENT PURGE SERIES

Don't miss out on the next book in the series! **Visit the following link and I'll let you know when it's available!**
http://mcbassauthor.com/letmeknow

Book 0 - Harbinger
Book 1 - Awakening
Book 2 - Evolution
Book 3 - Discovery (Coming soon)